Painting Water